ADVENTURES IN FRONTIER AMERICA

FRONTIER FARMER

Kansas Adventures

by Catherine E. Chambers

Illustrated by Len Epstein

Troll Associates

Library of Congress Cataloging in Publication Data

Chambers, Catherine E.
  Frontier farmer.

  (Adventures in frontier America)
  Summary: When Matt's father dies in 1881, he and his
mother decide to stay on their Kansas homestead despite
the perils of life on that frontier.
  [1. Frontier and pioneer life—Kansas—Fiction.
2. Kansas—Fiction] I. Epstein, Len, ill. II. Title.
III. Series: Chambers, Catherine E. Adventures in
frontier America.
PZ7.C3558Frf 1984   [Fic]   83-18279
ISBN 0-8167-0053-2 (lib. bdg.)
ISBN 0-8167-0054-0 (pbk.)

10   9   8   7   6   5   4   3   2   1

FRONTIER FARMER

Kansas Adventures

After Pa died in 1881, Matt Foster thought he and Ma would have to go back East. He should have known his mother better.

"We've put two years of our lives into this homestead," Ma said. Her black eyes snapped. "Kansas hasn't seen the last of us! This is our *home!*"

Home was a wooden house that Pa had built to replace the "soddy," or sod house, in which they had first lived. The new house had three rooms. It was very plain, but it was beautiful to Matt and Ma. Matt also loved the barn and the strong hard-working horses. He liked the two patient cows he milked every day. The barn had a tiger cat and her kittens to keep out mice. It also had a mower, a thresher, and a packer. The Fosters were very proud of them. Matt was worried, though. He was just thirteen. Was he going to be able to take Pa's place? Was he big enough to be a frontier homesteader?

These were the years of the settling of America's frontier. Until 1862, the frontier had really been two strips of land separated by hundreds of miles. One frontier included all the land west of the original thirteen colonies to Iowa, Missouri, and Arkansas.

America's other frontier was the strip of land between the Pacific Ocean and the Rocky Mountains. A "Great Migration" to Oregon and California had taken place. In Oregon, farmers came from the East to settle on the rich farmland. At the same time, "California fever" brought gold prospectors and adventurers to California.

All the lands between these two frontiers were known as the Great Plains. This land was also called the "Great American Desert." Farmers thought that no crops would grow there because there were no trees. That is why there were so few settlers in this territory.

This changed in 1862, when Congress passed the Homestead Act. This said that any adult who would settle the open land could have it free. All a farmer had to do was "prove" he meant to live on it himself. That meant planting crops, building a house, and living in it for five

years. After that the government gave the farmer a deed of ownership. The railroad companies also gave land they owned to settlers who would homestead on it. The railroad companies believed they could profit by transporting goods and passengers between settlements on the plains. Now thousands of people had a chance to become landowners even though they were not rich. That was how the Fosters came to Kansas.

Last year Pa started plowing as soon as the ground thawed. Matt helped him. It took both of them to get the plowing and planting done.

In late summer Pa had hired laborers to help with the harvest. Farmhands who didn't own land often wandered through the West doing such work. "I hope we can make it on our own till harvest time," Ma said to Matt hopefully.

"Sure we can, Ma," Matt answered. But he was worried. The land was good, and it was already cleared. But last year it took both Pa and Matt to plow and plant

8

it. This year Ma followed the plow, dropping the seed into the fresh-turned furrows. They worked from dawn to dark. When the first wheat came up, the cows knocked down the fence and trampled it. Ma looked at Matt across the supper table, her shoulders sagging.

"I'll put an ad in the papers in Wichita and Abilene: 'Farmer wanted. Experienced. Permanent. Can live in barn.' "

One day Matt was working by the river when a wagon came along the trail. A giant of a man was driving. He had a friendly smile. Beside him was a thin wiry boy who looked full of mischief. Matt liked him at once. The man took off his hat. "Afternoon, young man. I'm Mr. William Walter Lee, and this is my son Abraham. We're looking for M. S. Foster, who advertised for a farmer."

"That's my ma," Matt said. He ran to get her.

Mr. Lee had been born a field slave in Virginia. He knew a lot about farming. When he told Ma how he could put up barbed wire to keep the cows out of the fields, she hired him fast. After that, work on the homestead went more smoothly.

Matt and Abe became friends at once. Abe knew all kinds of stories about life further west. He swore he'd seen Buffalo Bill shoot a squirrel right between the eyes. During the day, Matt and Abe worked in the fields together whenever they weren't in school. Ma and Mr. Lee both set great store by school.

"Be glad you *can* go," Mr. Lee told Abe. "If you were a slave, you wouldn't be allowed to. But you're free, and you can read and write. Learning's a privilege. Don't you forget it!"

"That goes for you, too, Matt," Ma said firmly.

Sometimes they had to stay home to work. Most days they went to school and worked hard there, too. Matt thought Abe's stories were more exciting than the ones

10

they read in school. On warm nights, Matt sneaked out of
the loft and Abe sneaked out of the barn. They lay on their
backs down by the river and whispered about being cow-
boys and going to Dodge City. The West was really wild
there! Long-mustached Wild Bill Hickok was the marshal.
There were noisy hotels filled with action and excitement.
Matt and Abe longed to see Dodge City, but their parents
wouldn't even let them go to Wichita.

"You have enough trouble to get into here," Ma said
firmly. "And enough work to keep your thoughts off mischief." That was certainly true! Especially when harvest
time came. Ma went into town looking for extra workers
but came back frowning. "I couldn't find anyone. We'll
have to get the crops in ourselves."

"My pa thinks the men don't want to work for a lady," Abe told Matt. "They think you're going to have to give up your claim."

Mr. Lee and Matt and Abe worked and worked. But they couldn't keep up with the crops. One morning when they went to breakfast, the kitchen was empty. Porridge was steaming. Coffee was boiling, but Ma wasn't there. Matt made the flapjacks. Ma still didn't appear. Mr. Lee and the boys got worried and went to look for her. The McCormick reaper wasn't in the barn. They found Ma driving it across a far field. She was doing a good job, too, and she knew it.

"My pa taught me once, when I was young. Guess you never forget how." After that, Ma worked in the fields all day, too, and the crops came in on time.

"I guess we showed folks," Ma said, rubbing her sore arms.

Not all the people around the Foster place were farmers. Many cattle ranchers had discovered Kansas had good grazing land. During cattle drives from the far West, herds were fattened up in Kansas before being sold. Before long,

ranchers staked claims and built ranch houses in Kansas. That way, their cattle didn't have to make the long trip along the Chisholm and Santa Fe Trails. The huge herds needed thousands of acres to graze on. The ranchers didn't buy all that land or homestead it. Instead they owned the "spread" where their ranch house stood. They let their herds roam over the open government lands. But now homesteaders like the Fosters were staking claims and starting farms on this land.

Farms needed fences to keep cattle and other animals out of planted fields. Often these fences ran right across the ranchers' cattle runs. Some ranchers thought that work that couldn't be done on horseback wasn't worth doing. They looked down on farmers and called them "nesters." Farmers were building nests on the open land. Cowhands thought life in the open was better than life in houses. And those fences sure got in the way! Why didn't farmers stay back East and leave the range to the cowmen?

Matt knew the ranchers around the Foster place were waiting to see if Ma would give up the claim. Mr. Matheson and the other ranchers had liked Pa. They liked Ma and Matt, too. When Pa died, Mr. Matheson offered to buy out Pa's claim. He didn't think a widow and boy could last out the next three years. Ma never talked about it. But Matt and Abe did.

Often the Matheson cattle knocked down the Fosters' wooden fences. "They didn't do it on purpose," Ma always said. When Mr. Lee put up the new barbed-wire fence, that couldn't happen any more.

One morning in the summer of 1882, Mr. Lee came galloping up to Ma. "Mrs. Foster, somebody cut the wires down by the river. Most of the south fields have been trampled."

"You don't think Mr. Matheson did it?"

"Sure looks like it—or somebody who wants to get a herd to water. The river runs right through your land there. Cowhands used to go there all the time before we fenced it."

Planting those fields had been backbreaking work for Ma. She went straight into the house and cleaned herself up. "Saddle Bessie for me," she shouted to Matt. She came out all dressed up and tore across the fields toward the Matheson place.

"Mr. Matheson swears he didn't do it. He said he'd give orders to his men to stay away," said Ma when she returned. Her eyes were still snapping as she dished up supper.

"Do you believe him?" Matt asked.

"Yes. But that doesn't mean his cowhands didn't do it on their own—or some other rancher!"

"It could be night riders," suggested Matt.

"Matt Foster, this is not Dodge City! I just don't want to hear such ideas!"

Matt and Abe talked about the night riders a lot. Stories about them were sweeping across the prairie. All

through nester territory, both nesters and ranchers were putting up barbed wire. Often they put it up across each other's land, or across what the cowhands thought ought to be their land. At night armed men rode out with bandannas across their faces. They cut down each other's wire. Often there were shootings.

Matt didn't want to frighten Ma, but he was sure that was what was happening here.

The wire down by the river was cut again. Ma's face got grimmer. Two weeks went by. It happened once more.

Matt talked to Abe. "How do we know it isn't night riders? We ought to keep watch!"

"You know what your Ma will say. And my Pa!"

"So we won't tell them." Ma was used to the boys sleeping out on summer nights. She didn't need to know that now they slept by the river and took their hunting rifles!

For a week nothing happened. Then one night Matt sat up suddenly. A steady thudding was coming across the prairie. It was the sound of a thousand hoofs. Moonlight shone on the horns of cattle. Metal glinted on gun barrels. The figures on horseback seemed to have no faces. *Night riders!*

Matt poked Abe and put a hand over his mouth so he would not cry out. They both jumped up. Matt's heart was pounding. The shadows of the haystack hid them.

Snap! The night riders cut the wires. The cattle poured through into the Foster field. *"Keep out!"* Matt shouted. He fired his gun into the air. Lanterns flared. Then flames leaped high. *The haystack was on fire!* Matt started to run. He bumped into Abe. Arms like iron caught him. He fought wildly. Then he saw that it was Mr. Lee.

"Get to the corral, both of you! Fast! We'll hold them off there." The deep voice was a harsh whisper. Matt and the Lees streaked for the corral. Ma was there, fully dressed, carrying her rifle. *They've been keeping watch, too,* thought Matt. *Ma and Mr. Lee. They never told us.*

The herd was trampling all the fields. The men on horseback urged them on. Ma swung her rifle up. "No night riders are driving us off our land!" She fired into the air. A night rider's rifle blazed in answer. With a bellow of pain, one of the cows in the corral fell over.

Matt didn't even know what he was doing. His gun came up, and he fired at the figure. The man cried out and clutched his shoulder. His rifle dropped.

Suddenly, the night riders were gone. Their herd slowly followed.

I shot a man, Matt thought. His breathing hurt him.

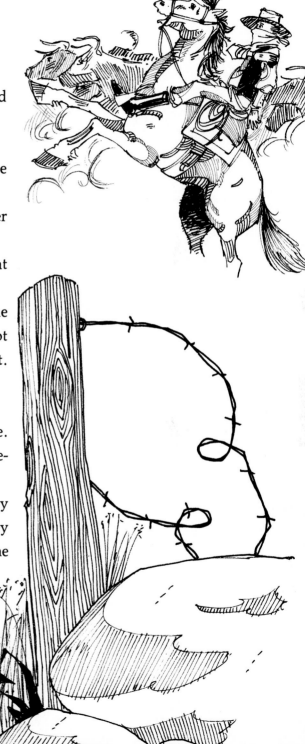

More horesmen came galloping from the opposite direction. Matt swung round. Mr. Lee lifted his rifle.

"Hold your fire!" It was Mr. Matheson and other neighbors. "We saw the fire. What happened?"

"Are you sure you don't know?" Matt said straight at him.

"Night riders?" Mr. Matheson looked at Ma. She nodded. He looked Matt right in the eyes. "When I shoot my gun I don't wear a mask. And I don't strike at night. But I promise you we'll find out who does."

They galloped off across the moonlit prairie.

No one slept the rest of the night. Ma made coffee. They were all still up when dawn lit the sky. Mr. Matheson returned.

"We got them. Thanks to your boy's good shot. They were punchers up from the Chisholm Trail. Thought they could drive you farmers off the range and put the blame on me and the other ranchers."

"Did I kill the man?" Matt asked fearfully. Mr. Matheson shook his head.

"Just winged him. But it slowed the others down. We locked them in the town jail. Marshal Colby will tend to them when he returns."

Matt and Abe wanted to ride to town to see the prisoners, but Ma put her foot down. "There's been enough trouble already. And look at all the work we have to do!"

They worked until they thought they would drop. But that night, out in the field, Abe rolled over and looked at Matt. "You thinking what I'm thinking?"

Matt nodded. Silently, they sneaked their favorite horse out of the corral. Silently, they climbed up bareback. They didn't start galloping till they were out of earshot.

In town they were quiet as mice again. They slid off the horse and crept toward the jail. A strange thing was happening. Men were bringing out the prisoners, who were bound and gagged. The men lifted the prisoners onto horses. Then mounted men led the prisoners past the end

of the town's wooden walkway. Matt and Abe followed in
the shadows.

Just beyond the last building was a giant tree. Ropes
hung down. Matt gasped.

The sound was heard! A voice said sharply, "Some-body's here!" Matt and Abe crouched down quickly. The lantern-light swung toward them. Someone said, "Well, I'll be!" It was Mr. Matheson. He hauled the boys out by their collars. "What are you two doing here?"

"Please, sir, we just wanted to find out what's going on."

"It's no place for you. Get along home." Mr. Matheson let go of them and forced a smile. "You did your share of the work last night. We're going to hold a necktie party, that's all."

Abe's voice whispered in Matt's ear. *"He means a hanging!"*

"But you can't do that!" Matt cried out. "There hasn't been a trial. That's against the law."

"We're the law here, son," Mr. Matheson said with kind firmness. "The government's so far away. The folks who live here have a duty to keep order. Just like you took care of your ma and your homestead the other night. We have to make sure things like that don't happen again."

"Come on!" somebody shouted. "We've got business to take care of!"

The boys were pushed aside. The cowmen's horses were led toward the great tree. Matt threw himself forward. Somebody's arm caught him. Somebody else was holding Abe.

All at once a kind of cyclone exploded in the crowd. It was a wagon, kicking up dust. A shaft of moonlight hit it. *There was Ma.* And Mr. Lee. Mr. Lee saw the boys and dove for them. The men holding them let go in a hurry. Ma stood in the wagon and raised her rifle. She fired it straight up in the air. That got attention fast.

"What do you boys think you're up to?" She didn't mean Matt and Abe, she meant the crowd.

"Mrs. Foster, this ain't no place for a lady," Mr. Matheson said.

"We came looking for our sons," Ma snapped back. "And a good thing, too. We found the jail empty and guessed what you were up to. Have you gone clear out of your minds?"

A man cleared his throat. "Excuse me for saying so, Mrs. Foster, but this is not your business."

"It is my business! That was my cow that was killed, and those were my fields that were trampled. Or are you forgetting that?"

Mr. Matheson tried to calm Ma. "That's why you should want to see justice done. We all have to look after our rights and property."

"Of course I want justice! But that means the law, not necktie parties! I guess the cowmen thought they were looking out for their rights, too. My homestead's in the way of their cattle drive." Ma looked from one face to another. "Don't you see? These men have to go on trial so a jury can decide. Otherwise where will all this end? My boy shot a man last night. He was trying to protect our livestock. Suppose that man had died? And suppose his friends had come for this kind of justice? Would it have been all right for them to string Matt up? Can't you see that's exactly the same thing?"

There was a silence. Men moved uneasily. Mr. Lee jumped up on the wagon and took out his knife. "I aim to cut these men down and get them back behind bars.

Anyone helping, or am I going to do it all myself?"

Grumbling, the mob broke up. Three men helped Mr. Lee undo the nooses. The prisoners were thrown into the wagon with Mr. Lee and the boys to guard them. Ma drove like lightning back to the jail.

"Won't be any more trouble now," Mr. Lee said. "But we'd better stay till morning all the same."

In the morning, Marshal Colby returned to town with two deputies. They took the cowmen to another town for trial. Later the marshal came by the homestead. "There are six good cows in town waiting for you to collect them. They were sent to you by the owner of that cattle herd. That's part of the fine the jury decided on." So the Fosters now had more livestock than before.

Matt and Abe rebuilt the fences. Mr. Lee and Ma worked to save what they could of the fields.

The next cattle drive didn't ask for trouble. They may have heard about what had happened. The leader came to the house and asked politely if they could bed down by the river. Ma said yes. She even sent the men a fresh-baked cake. After the cattle drive moved on, Mr. Lee came back from the river with a broad grin.

"Look what they left behind!"

He had a newborn calf under each arm. "Must have been born during the night. They were left because they couldn't walk fast enough."

"One for each boy," Ma laughed. She looked at Matt and Abe. "You can have them if you can raise them. They'll have to be fed from bottles for a while."

"Now the Lees own livestock," Abe said proudly.

Mr. Lee decided he wanted to homestead, too. Some land was still open not far away. He could live in a tent or soddy there and still work on the Foster farm.

"You and Abe can still sleep in our barn during winter if you want to," Ma said. "You can borrow our plow and mower till you get your own."

Little by little, the open land was being filled. More and more of the new homesteaders were farmers. The days of the open cattle range were coming to an end.

On June 25, 1884, the Fosters celebrated five years on their homestead. Their claim was now "proved." Ma put on her best dress and bonnet, Matt wore his good vest and a tie. They and the Lees drove to the land claims office. Mr. Matheson met them there, to serve as a witness. He told the clerk Ma had been living and working the claim for five whole years. Ma signed some papers and paid a fee. The clerk handed her the deed of ownership.

"I'm going to take it home and hang it next to Pa's picture," Ma said happily. That night there was a big party at the Foster farm. Farmers and ranchers came from miles around. Abe played his fiddle and everybody danced.

It's taken time and lots of hard work, but Pa's dream has come true, thought Matt. *But best of all, I've helped to make it come true—I'm a frontier farmer—and proud of it!*